Paper Play

Published by SpiceBox™
12171 Horseshoe Way,
Richmond, BC,
Canada V7A 4V4

First published in 2011
Copyright © SpiceBox™ 2011
Text and photographs copyright © SpiceBox™

ISBN 10: 1-926567-33-1
ISBN 13: 978-1-926567-33-4

CEO and Publisher: Ben Lotfi
Editor: Trisha Pope
Creative Director: Garett Chan
Art Director: Christine Covert
Projects and Templates: Alice Clair
Design and Layout: Alice Clair
Production: James Badger
Sourcing: Janny Lam
Photography: Charmaine Muzyka and Alice Clair
Illustration: Charmaine Muzyka

Special thank you to our models Jennifer Blanco, Silvia Beck,
Cameron Attwell, and Gizmo Clair.

For more SpiceBox products and information, visit our website:
www.spicebox.ca

Printed in China

1 3 5 7 9 10 8 6 4 2

Table of Contents

Introduction

Crafting with paper is a popular activity that has been around for ages. In fact it probably dates back right to the invention of paper, in China in the 2nd century BC! It's success is likely because there is something immensely satisfying about taking a piece of paper, snipping it up with a pair of scissors, and then gluing the pieces back together again, creating a new and exciting shape.

Making creations with paper is a wonderful activity for any time and for people of all ages; there are so many things you can do with it. You can cut and glue it, draw and paint on it, fold it, staple it, and even sew it. It comes in so many styles, colors and patterns that the things that you can make with paper are as limitless as your imagination.

In this book we want to give you lots of projects to keep you busy and having fun, but also that act as an inspiration for your own paper crafting ideas. Most of the projects can be adapted and changed to suit your imagination, and all of them can be decorated however you wish. Paper crafting is a fun and rewarding pastime, so let's get started!

Materials:

To make the projects in this book you are going to need:

Scissors: a pair for cutting paper, not mom's sewing scissors!

Glue: regular white glue, like the type used at school. A glue stick is also handy, if you have one.

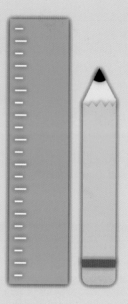

Ruler and pencil: are handy for drawing lines.

Paper folding tool: this is a useful tool for paper crafting. You can use the tool in two ways. The first is to score lines in the paper to help you create straight and even folds. To "score" means to create a dent in the surface of the paper. You will notice it will be much easier to fold the paper along a line that you have scored, and this is particularly helpful when you are folding small pieces of paper.

The other way you can use the tool is to help you create a crisp fold by pressing the fold down with the edge of the tool. Once you have scored a line in the paper and folded it, run the edge of the tool along the fold to make it nice and flat. Maybe you've run your thumbnail along a fold before, to make it a sharp – this is a tool to do the same thing. It is particularly helpful when you have to fold a piece of paper over on itself a few times and it becomes too thick to flatten easily.

Clear sticky tape: like Scotch® tape, is used on some of the projects.

Double-stick tape: the kind that is sticky on both sides is also a quick way to attach pieces together.

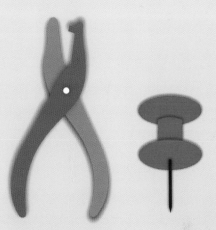

Small hole punch: is used in some of the projects. You can also pierce a hole in a piece of paper with a thumbtack. Do this by placing your paper on top of a mouse pad or other soft surface, and then push the tack through the paper to make the hole.

Brads: or paper fasteners, these are the little round brass pins with arms that spread open flat to secure pieces of paper together.

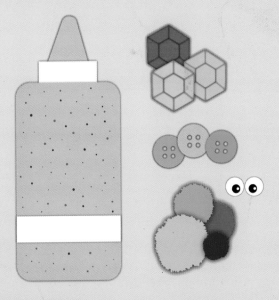

Decorative items: most of the projects in this book will be a bit more exciting if you use your own imagination and supplies to decorate them. You can paint, glitter, sticker, feather, pompom, or draw your decorations on. Put together any supplies you have that can be used in paper crafting, and then let your imagination run wild!

Black marker: is used for drawing in details.

Transferring Patterns:

This book and kit come with a number of pattern sheets to help you make your projects. We recommend that you scan or photocopy all of them and save them so that you can make the projects again or print out an extra pattern set to make with a friend.

In some cases the patterns can be cut out directly from the sheet. Otherwise you will want to transfer the patterns onto a piece of craft paper. You can transfer using the following method:

1 Take a piece of tracing paper, and lay it over the pattern you wish to trace. You may want to tape it down so that it doesn't shift position while you are tracing.

2 Trace over each of the shapes on the pattern sheet.

3 Gently flip the tracing paper over and lightly rub along the lines with the side of your pencil.

Back

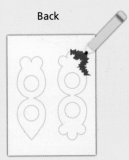

4 Turn your tracing paper back over so the pattern is on the top again, lay it over the card stock you wish to use for your project, and retrace over the lines that you drew. The pencil lead you rubbed onto the back of the paper will transfer onto the cardstock, leaving the pattern that you traced.

Front

Another option: If your parents have carbon or graphite paper, follow steps 1 and 2. Then, take your tracing paper and place it onto the cardstock you want to use. Slip the piece of carbon or graphite paper between the tracing paper and cardstock (with the carbon side down) and retrace your pattern.

Now you know how to transfer your pattern, and your materials are assembled, so let's get crafting!

These puppets are easy to make, and staging a shadow puppet show is a wonderfully imaginative activity for kids of all ages!

Shadow Puppets

Materials

Loose template sheets:
Pirate Shadow Puppets

Thin wooden dowels   Tape   Brads

Method

1 Punch out the puppet templates and punch holes at the joints, where marked.

2 Join the limbs to the puppets with brads.

3 Tape thin wooden dowels to the back of the puppet pieces. Keep in mind how you want to move the puppets. You may want to attach a piece of doweling to each of the jointed arms so you can move them independently to create movement in the puppet, or simply attach the dowel to the main part of the puppet.

Back

4 Create a shadow puppet stage by hanging a white sheet in a door frame. Turn a small table on its side behind the sheet for you to hide behind and use as the stage for your puppets. Aim a desk light with a bendable neck at the sheet above the table, from behind. The light will cause the puppets to cast shadows through the sheet. Stage your performance and entertain your guests!

Time to play princess for the day! These super-easy crowns and tiaras are just the thing for small royalty.

Tiara and Crown

Materials

Patterns from book: Crown and Tiara page 69, 70 | Cardstock | Tracing paper and pencil | Ruler | Scissors | Glue | Stapler | Glitter glue, gems, buttons, or other embellishments

Method

CROWN

1 Transfer the crown pattern onto card stock and cut the piece out. Then cut out a 1 3/4" x 12" head band for your crown.

2 Glue the crown piece you cut out to one end of the head band, lining them up along the bottom edges and let the piece dry.

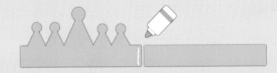

3 Decorate the crown with glitter glue, felt pens, buttons, gems, etc.

4 Wrap the crown around your head and hold it into place where the band overlaps. Carefully slide it off your head and staple or glue the band together.

TIARA

1 Transfer the tiara pattern onto card stock and cut the piece out. Then cut out a 1 3/4" x 12" head band for your tiara.

2 Glue the tiara shape onto one end of head band, lining them up along the bottom edges and let the piece dry.

3 Decorate the tiara with glitter glue, felt pens, buttons, gems, etc.

4 Wrap the tiara around your head and hold it into place where the band overlaps. Carefully slide it off your head and staple or glue the band together.

These cute little pencil pals will keep you company while you practice your writing!

Pencil Toppers

Materials

Loose pattern sheet: Pencil Toppers

Scissors

Glue

Tape

Pencils to decorate

Method

1 Cut out each pattern and fold it in half. For the fox, fold the pattern in half before cutting out the section between the ears.

2 Cut a strip of paper about an inch wide, and wrap it around the top of a pencil, taping it closed. It should be fairly tight, but you should still be able to slide the paper tube off the pencil.

3 Dot glue on each side of the paper tube, and place the pencil topper over the tube, pressing down gently so that it adheres to the paper tube on both sides. Once it is dry, you can slide the topper on and off the pencil.

Bookmarks

Materials

Patterns from book: Bookmarks page 61, 62   Cardstock (black, orange, yellow, white, gray, pink)   Tracing paper and pencil   Scissors   Glue   Tape   Black pen or marker   Googly eyes

Method

TIGER

1 Use the Bookmark pattern to trace the following pieces:
- a. Bookmark base x 1 (orange)
- b. Snout x 1 (yellow)
- c. Teeth x 2 (white)
- d. Stripes x 4 (black)
- e. Nose x 1 (black)
- f. Outer ear x 2 (orange)
- g. Inner ear x 2 (black)

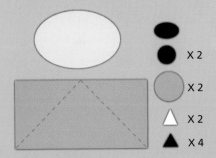

2 Fold the corners of the orange bookmark base along the fold marks shown in the diagram, creating a triangle. Use a piece of tape to tape these two pieces together.

Back

3 Turn the bookmark over and glue the snout onto the front, then glue the black nose onto the snout.

4 Glue a black inner ear onto each orange ear and then glue the completed ears to the bookmark from the back side.

5 Glue the teeth onto the bottom of the snout.

6 Glue the 4 stripes onto the front of tiger. Use a black marker to add eyes and whisker details.

ELEPHANT

1 Use the Bookmark pattern to trace the following pieces:
- a. Base x 1 (gray)
- b. Trunk x 1 (gray)
- c. Outer ears x 2 (gray)
- d. Inner ears x 2 (pink)
- e. Tusks x 2 (white)

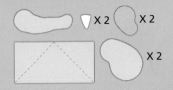

2 Fold the corners of the gray bookmark base down, along the fold lines shown in the diagram, creating a triangle. Use tape to tape these two pieces together.

Back

3 Turn the bookmark over and glue the gray trunk onto bookmark base and then add the tusks.

4 Assemble the ears by gluing the pink inner ears onto each gray outer ear, and then glue the ears onto the back of the bookmark.

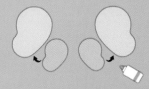

5 Use a black marker to add eyes or use googly eyes.

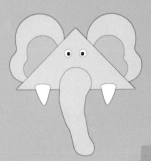

Robot Toy

Materials

Loose pattern
sheet: Robot

Ruler

Folding
tool

Scissors

Glue

2 googly eyes
(optional)

2 Brads
(optional)

Method

1 Take the pattern sheet for the Robot, and use a ruler and the folding tool to score along the fold lines. Cut out the pattern pieces and fold along the lines you scored, pressing them down with the folding tool.

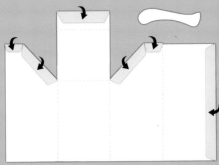

2 Fold the arm pieces along the fold line, and dot together with glue.

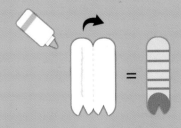

3 Make sure the tabs on the main body piece are folded in, and dot them with glue. Assemble the robot body by folding it along the scored lines, gently pressing the sides onto the glued tabs to fix into place.

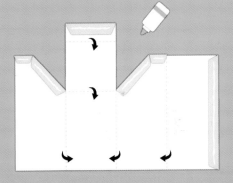

4 Attach the arms to the sides of the robot with glue or gently push brads through the arms and the body to create moveable arms.

5 Glue on the googly eyes if you are using them.

21

Perhaps not the scariest of all the dinosaurs, this paperosaurus is still happy to stand guard for you while you work!

Dinosaur Toy

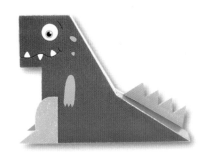

Materials

Loose pattern sheet: Dinosaur   Ruler   Folding tool   Scissors   Glue   2 googly eyes (optional)

Method

1 Place the pattern sheet for the Dinosaur on the table and using a ruler and folding tool, score on the fold lines. Cut the pattern out, including the slit in the tail, and fold on the score lines, pressing the folds down with the folding tool.

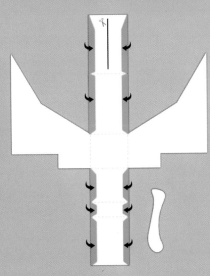

2 Fold both leg pieces in half on the fold lines and glue them together to create two double-sided legs.

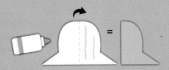

3 Fold the spikes in half and glue, but don't glue the tabs together. It may be easier to cut out the sections between the spikes after you have folded and glued them.

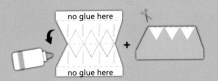

no glue here

no glue here

4 Slide folded spikes through the slit in the tail. Unfold the tabs on the spikes and glue them to the underside of the tail to fasten the spikes into place.

5 Assemble the dinosaur body by folding it up along the scored lines, gluing the sides down onto the tabs.

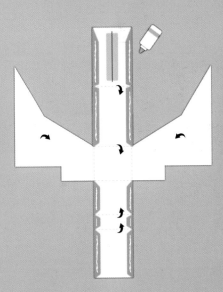

6 Attach the legs to the front sides of the monster with glue.

7 Glue on the googly eyes if you are using them.

23

No need to be afraid of the dark when you have these sweet switch plate covers watching over you!

Light Switch Covers

Materials

Patterns from book: Girl and Penguin Light Switch Covers page 60, 61

Cardstock (black, brown, white, red, pink, peach, yellow)

Tracing paper and pencil

Scissors

Glue

Double-sided tape

Googly eyes

Gems or glitter glue (optional)

Method

PENGUIN

1 Transfer the Penguin patterns onto cardstock using the technique on page 11.

Use black for the body, white for the inner body, yellow for the feet and red for the bow tie.

2 Cut out all of the shapes; don't forget to cut out the spaces for the switch to poke through. If your light switch looks different from the one in the photo, then ask an adult to help you adjust the rectangle cut outs to match the size of your switch.

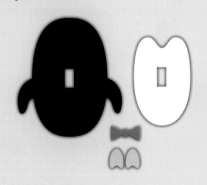

3 Glue the inner body onto the outer body, lining up openings for the switch. Glue the feet to the back of the outer body, and then glue the bow tie below the opening for the switch.

4 Glue on googly eyes.

5 The easiest way to attach the cover to the light switch plate is with double-sided tape. Ask an adult to help you with this part!

GIRL

1 Transfer Girl patterns onto cardstock using peach for the face, pink for the cheeks and the bow, the mouth in white and the hair on yellow, brown, or black.

2 Cut out all of the shapes; don't forget to cut out the spaces for the switch to poke through. If your light switch looks different from the one in the photo, then ask an adult to help you adjust the rectangle cut outs to match the size of your switch.

3 Assemble the switch plate cover using glue, attaching the mouth and cheeks first, then the hair, and finally adding the bow and googly eyes for decoration.

4 Ask an adult to help you attach the cover to the light switch plate with double-sided tape.

These funky frames dress up any look! Add a bit of sparkle with gemstones and feathers. Lovely!

Glasses

Materials

Loose pattern sheets: Glasses | Thick card stock | Ruler | Folding tool | Scissors | Glue-stick and white craft | Gems, feathers, glitter glue and other embellishments

Method

1 To make your glasses extra sturdy and help them last longer, glue the sheet with the glasses pattern on it, onto a second sheet of cardstock. This is best done with a glue stick so that the paper doesn't wrinkle up when it dries. Be generous with the glue stick when gluing the pattern sheet to the card stock sheet, so that the pieces of paper don't separate after you cut out the glasses.

2 Score using a ruler and the folding tool along the score lines.

3 Ask an adult to help you carefully cut out the eyeholes, then the outside of the glasses and the arms.

4 Fold over the tabs on the sides of the glasses and attach the arms with glue.

5 Decorate with gems and embellishments to create a funky fashion statement!

In need of a clever disguise, worthy of Clark Kent? These smashing glasses will do the trick, fooling your friends every time!

Disguise

Materials

Loose pattern sheet: Disguise

Thick card stock

Ruler

Folding tool

Scissors

Glue-stick and white craft

Method

1 To make your glasses extra sturdy and help them last longer, glue the sheet with the glasses pattern on it, onto a second sheet of cardstock. This is best done with a glue stick so that the paper doesn't wrinkle up when it dries. Be generous with the glue stick when gluing the pattern sheet to the card stock sheet, so that the pieces of paper don't separate after you cut out the glasses.

2 Score using a ruler and the folding tool along the score lines.

3 Ask an adult to help you carefully cut out the eyeholes, then the outside of the glasses and the arms.

4 Fold over the tabs on the sides of the glasses and attach the arms with glue.

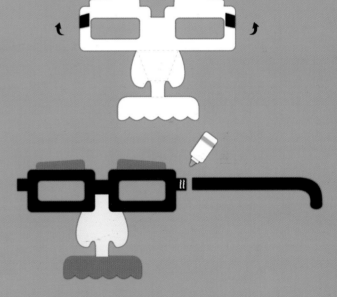

5 Bend the nose and mustache, creasing with the folding tool.

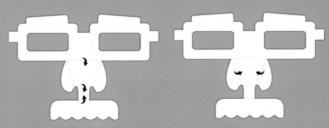

29

These fabulous toy cars may not go very fast, but they sure look stylish!

Toy Cars

Materials

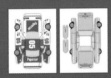
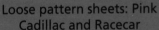

Loose pattern sheets: Pink Cadillac and Racecar   Ruler   Folding tool   Scissors   Glue

Method

RACECAR:

1 Lay the pattern sheet flat on the table and using a ruler and paper folding tool, score lines along all of the dotted fold lines on the pattern.

2 Cut out the pattern and fold and press firmly on the score marks with the folding tool.

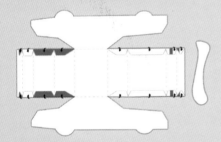

3 Assemble the car by gluing along each of the tabs and pressing them onto the side panels of the car's body.

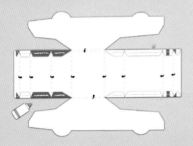

PINK CADILLAC

1 Use the folding tool to score lines on all the fold lines on the pattern sheet.

2 Cut out the car pattern and the two wings.

3 Dab a bit of glue on the back of each of the wings, and then fold them in half along the score lines.

Front   Back

4 Glue the wings onto the body of the car as indicated in the diagram below – one on each side of the rear of the car.

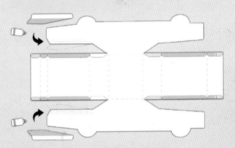

5 Assemble the body of the car, gluing the tabs to the side panels of the car. The wings should now be pointing up from the back of the car.

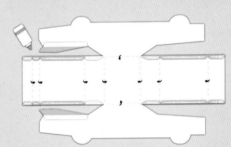

31

When there is a battle between the cats and the dogs, fur will fly! Who will win this game of tic-tac-toe?

Tic-Tac-Paw

Materials

Loose template sheets: Cat and Dog Tic-Tac-Toe

Folding tool

Scissors

Glue

Method

1 Using the folding tool, score along all of the dotted fold lines, and then cut out each of the pieces for the cat and dog cubes; there are 5 cubes per set.

2 Fold on each score line and press them flat with the side of the folding tool.

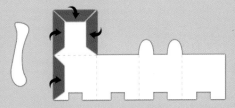

3 Assemble each animal cube by dotting glue along the tabs, and then folding the cubes onto the tabs- pressing gently to seal the edges.

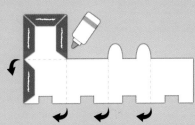

4 Cut out the game board template and challenge another player to a battle!

Bow Tie

Materials

Patterned paper:
1 square (6" x 6") and 2
rectangles, each 1" x 2"

Pencil

Ruler

Folding
tool

Scissors

Glue

Method

1 For the main bow tie piece, cut out a square of your favorite patterned paper, approximately 6" x 6".

2 On the back of the paper, draw a line every ½" using a ruler and pencil.

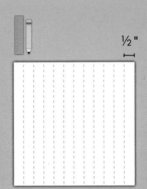

½ "

3 Using the folding tool and a ruler as a guide, score along each pencil line.

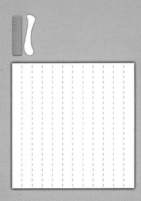

4 Starting at one end of the paper, fold back and forth on the lines, like an accordion.

5 Glue a 1"x2" strip of paper into a loop, and slide the folded paper through it.

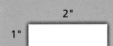

2"

1"

=

6 Fan out the pleats on either side of loop, creating a bow tie.

7 Take the other 1"x2" piece of paper and glue the top edge of it onto the back of the bow tie. Use this tab to tuck the bow tie into your shirt collar.

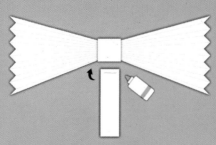

What girl doesn't love to dress up with lots of jewelry? Give them a touch of glam with some glitter glue and these fabulous pieces are sure to impress!

Paper Jewelry

Materials

Patterns from book:
Heart and Flower Rings
page 59

Colored
cardstock

Tracing paper
and pencil

Ruler

Folding
tool

Scissors

Glue

Glitter glue,
gems, pompoms

Method

HEART CHAIN NECKLACE

1 To make a chain necklace 36" long, cut 24 narrow strips of paper that are 4" long to make the hearts, and another 24 that are 3" long to make the loops. All of them should be the same width – about ½" wide.

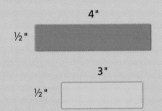

2 Fold each of the long (4") strips in half and then turn the ends inward so that they meet in the middle, creating a heart. Dot a bit of glue on the ends and press them together tightly to let glue dry. Do this with all of the long strips.

3 Now, take a short 3" strip and loop it through two hearts. Glue the ends together to create a loop. Continue with all of the short pieces to loop together the hearts you made, creating a chain.

4 Loop final 3" strip through first and last heart and glue it closed.

HEART/FLOWER RING

1 Transfer the ring patterns onto your chosen cardstock using the method described on page 11.

2 Use a ruler and the scoring tool, and score the fold lines as indicated in the diagram.

3 *You may want to get adult help for this as you will need to use scissors with a pointy end or a craft knife. Carefully cut out the inside circles of the rings. Try sliding your finger through the hole to see if it fits. If not, make the circles larger. Once the circle is the right size, finish cutting out the ring pieces.

4 Take each ring section and fold the ornament back along the line that you scored. Match up the halves of the rings, as per the diagrams, and glue the sections together.

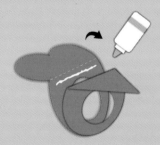

5 Decorate your rings with glitter glue, gems, or pompoms, and show off your new bling!

This lovely display of flowers will always stay as bright and fresh as a daisy! Place it on a windowsill to add cheer to any room.

Vase and Flowers

Materials

Colored cardstock: 10 squares - 4" x 4" and 10 squares – 3 ½" x 3 ½"

Patterned cardstock: 7" x 10"

Ruler

Folding tool

Scissors

Glue

Thumbtack

10 green pipe cleaners

Buttons, glitter glue, gems, or pompoms

Method

FLOWERS

1 Use a ruler and the folding tool to score all of the paper squares – both the 4" x 4" and 3½" x 3½" from corner to corner on both diagonals to create an X. Look at the diagram to help you with this.

2 Once all of the squares are scored, fold them in half along one diagonal score line, to make a large triangle, and then fold the triangle in half again along the second score line to make a smaller triangle. Press the folds flat with the folding tool.

3 Now, fold the triangle in half again to create an even smaller triangle – refer to the diagram – and press the fold flat.

4 Cut the bottom of the triangle off in a curve so that is rounded. Open the paper up and it should look like a flower with 8 petals. Do this to all the square papers, so that you have 10 large flower bases, and 10 smaller flower tops.

5 Stack one base and one flower top together, and poke a hole through the middle of them using a thumbtack on a soft surface (see page 9).

6 Insert a green pipe cleaner through the hole in the middle of the flowers, and bend the tip over to secure it in place. You may want to put a bit of glue on the underside of the flower where the pipe cleaner comes through, in order to secure them even more thoroughly.

7 Decorate middle of flowers with glitter glue, buttons, pompoms, or gems.

VASE

1 Cut a piece of cardstock that is 7" x 10".

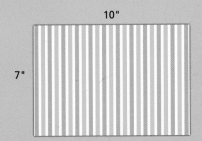

2 Run a thin line of glue along one of the short sides, and glue it to the opposite side, creating a tube. Hold it together for a moment, pressing down along the glue line until it has dried.

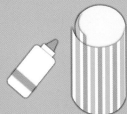

3 Stand the vase on the table and arrange the flowers in the vase to make a pretty centerpiece.

These adorable hats are just the thing for a fashion runway, or to accessorize a charming tea party outfit!

Mini Hats

Materials

Pattern from book: Hat Rim, Hat Top page 59

Cardstock (2 sheets of 8.5"x11" in desired colors)

Tracing paper and pencil

Ruler

Folding tool

Scissors

Glue

Elastic string or thin ribbon

Paper flowers or other embellishments

Method

1 Transfer the hat patterns onto cardstock (page 11), and cut out the pieces.

2 For the side of the hat: cut out a piece of cardstock that is 3"x11". Along each of the long sides, draw a line that is ½" from the edge. Score along each of these lines using your folding tool.

3 Once the two lines are scored, fold the top edge backward, and the bottom edge forward.

4 Unfold the two edges, and then carefully cut slits from the edge of the paper to the fold lines, ¼" apart, along the full length of the paper. Measure the first two or three cuts, and then judge the remaining cuts by sight, as they don't have to be perfectly spaced.

5 Bend the paper into a ring and glue the ends together to create the side of the hat. Refold the top tabs you just cut into the center of the hat, and the bottom tabs forward to the outside of the hat.

6 Dot glue onto each of the bottom tabs of the hat, and then slide the hat rim over the hat side, and press the tabs onto the underside of the hat rim, so that it is glued into place.

7 Set the hat top piece upside down on the table. Apply glue along the top tabs of the hat side, turn it upside down and carefully place it onto the hat top, pressing the tabs down from the inside of the hat to secure it in place.

8 Cut a 1"x11" strip from a coordinating colored or patterned paper.

9 Wrap the band around hat, pushing it down to sit flush against the hat rim, and glue it in place.

10 Using a small hole punch or push pin, poke a hole on each side of hat, where the band meets the rim. Thread elastic string through one hole and tie the end in a knot to secure it. Place your hat on your head and bring the string up under your chin to other hole and mark it when the length is correct. Thread it through the other hole until it meets the point you marked, and secure it with a knot. Cut off the extra length and tuck the loose ends under the hat band to hide them.

11 Decorate hat with paper flowers (see the instructions on page 41 for making paper flowers), glitter glue, feathers, etc.

Hang these cheerful characters from your door knob, and make them jump up and down for joy every time to enter your room!

Jumping Jacks

Materials

Loose pattern sheets: Jumping Jacks

Thick card stock

Scissors

Small hole punch

String or embroidery floss

8 Brads or metal fasteners

Googly eyes

Method

1 Cut out the pre-printed patterns of the bodies, arms and legs for the jumping jacks, and glue them onto cardstock. Cut the pieces out of the cardstock. This will make the pieces sturdier, so that your jumping jacks will not tear easily.

2 Punch a small hole on the pieces where they are marked. There are 5 holes on the body pieces, and two holes in each of the arms and the legs.

3 Line up the bottom hole in the right leg with the bottom right hole on the body piece. Insert a brad from the front, and fasten it through both the holes onto the back of the body. It needs to be loose enough for the leg to be able to swing freely.

4 Attach the rest of the limbs in the same way, fastening a brad through the body and the bottom hole each limb.

5 Cut two pieces of string about 6" long. Turn the jumping jack face down on the table, thread the first string through the top holes on both of the legs, and knot the ends of the string together. Snip off the loose ends.

6 Tie the arms together in the same way with the second piece of string threaded through the top holes, knotting the string together to create a loop.

7 Tie a long piece of string (12") around the loop of string between the legs, leaving enough length on one end of the string to tie it to the string between the arms. Leave the other end hanging down between the legs.

8 Tie a 4" piece of string through the hole in the top of the jumping jack to hang it.

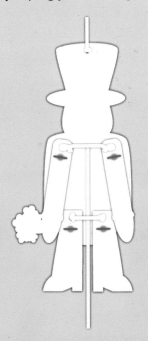

9 Use googly eyes on your jumping jack, if you wish, and color and decorate it.

10 Hold the top string in one hand and pull gently on the bottom string to make the arms and legs move!

The butterflies on this fluttering mobile will appear to be flying in circles in the breeze as it hangs in your room.

Butterfly Mobile

Materials

| Patterns from book: Butterflies page 64 | Patterned paper | Tracing paper and pencil | Ruler | Folding tool | Scissors | Glue | Clear fishing wire | Hole punch | One sheet of solid color cardstock 8.5x11 | Gems, buttons, glitter glue (optional) |

Method

1 Transfer the wing pattern onto your favorite patterned cardstock. For each butterfly, you will need 2 wings. On our mobile, we used 8 large butterflies, and 8 small butterflies, so we traced and cut out 16 large wings and 16 small wings.

2 Once all of your wings are cut out, score and fold each as per the pattern.

3 Cut 5 pieces of fishing line. 4 pieces should be approximately 20" long and 1 about 25" long.

4 Place one wing section flat on table with the pattern face down, and apply a thin line of glue down the middle of the butterfly, on the fold line.

5 Place the end of one piece of the fishing line along the glue line, and then carefully press another set of the same size wings on top of this, pattern side facing up. Try to line the top wings up with the bottom wings so that they are even.

6 Glue two more butterflies onto the piece of fishing line in this way, spacing them apart along the line.

7 When your first line is finished, make 3 other lines in the same way, and then on the longer line, glue 4 butterflies. After the butterflies are dry, open the wings up a bit more to make them look like they are flying.

8 Decorate the butterflies with rhinestones and glitter glue if you want, and let them dry thoroughly.

TO MAKE THE MOBILE

1 Cut two pieces of heavy cardstock that are 2" x 11". Measure 5½" along each of the strips, and at that point, cut a slit half way across the cardstock. See the diagram to help you with this.

	11"	
2"		1" Slit

✂

2 Slide one piece of cardstock over the other, at the slit that you just cut, so that they interlock.

3 Using a hole punch, punch two holes in the end of each strip, one at the top corner and one at the bottom corner.

4 Punch one hole along the bottom of one of the strips, near the centre of where they are joined.

5 Cut two pieces of fishing line that are each 20" long. Take one piece of line, and tie each end through the top holes on one of the strips of cardstock. Then, take the other line and tie each end to the top holes on the other piece of cardstock. You will be able to hang up your mobile at the point where the fishing line crosses in the middle.

6 Tie the top ends of the 3-butterfly lines to bottom holes on each end of the mobile base, and attach the 4-butterfly line to the middle hole.

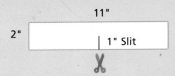

Do you dream of blasting off into space? This clever mobile will inspire your dreams of reaching the stars!

Space Mobile

Materials

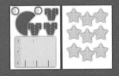

Loose pattern sheets: Space Ship and Stars · Ruler · Folding tool · Scissors · Glue · Clear fishing wire · Hole punch · 1 wooden dowel · Glitter glue (optional)

Method

1 Cut out all of the pieces from the pre-printed Space Ship and Stars sheets.

2 Fold each star in half vertically. Take three stars and glue one half of the first star to half of the second star. Then glue the remaining half of the second to half of the third star. Finally, glue the remaining half of the third star to the remaining half of the first star. Refer to the diagram and photo to help you with this. Glue all of the stars in the same way.

View From Top

3 Punch a small hole in the top of each star. Finish the stars by decorating them with glitter glue if you wish and set them aside while you make the rocket.

4 Punch holes on the body of the rocket where marked. Roll up the rocket body into a tube shape, and glue it together following the glue guides.

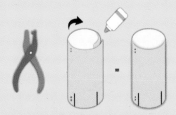

5 Create the nose of the rocket by turning the ends together to create a cone shape and glue the cone together along the glue guides.

6 Carefully apply a bead of glue around the rim of rocket (it is the end that doesn't have the slits) and attach the rocket nose. Hold it in place until the glue dries.

7 Score and fold the wing pieces on the fold lines. Glue them closed, being careful not to get any glue on the wing tabs.

8 Slide the wings through the slits on the rocket body. Fold back the tabs to secure the wings into place, and glue them down on the inside of your rocket.

9 Cut 5 pieces of fishing line of different lengths. Tie one piece through the hole in each of the stars, and tie two pieces through the holes in the rocket. You may want to stick down the ends with a bit of tape on the inside of the rocket.

10 To assemble your mobile, tie the rocket onto a piece of doweling and adjust it so that the nose is pointing up, a bit higher than the tail. Once you are happy with the placement of the rocket, add the stars, tying them on at different heights along the rod. Tie one piece of fishing line to either end of dowel to hang it up.

THE TALE OF BENJAMIN BUNNY
THE TALE OF THE FLOPSY BUNNIES
THE TALE OF JEMIMA PUDDLE-DUCK
THE TAILOR OF GLOUCESTER
THE TALE OF MR. JEREMY FISHER
THE TALE OF TWO BAD MICE
THE TALE OF PETER RABBIT
THE TALE OF TIMMY TIPTOES
THE TALE OF TOM KITTEN

Family and friends will love to receive a photo of you in one of these cheerful frames!

Photo Frames

Materials

Loose pattern sheet: Beach and Sports Embellishments

8½" x 11" piece of cardstock

Ruler

Folding tool

Scissors

Glue

Glitter glue or other embellishments (optional)

Method

1 Cut out an 8½" x 6" piece of cardstock, and fold it in half to make a 4¼" x 6" rectangle.

2 Unfold the card, and on the bottom half of the sheet, use a ruler and your folding tool to score a line ½" in from both edges, and down from the fold line. Finally, score a line ¾" up from the bottom edge.

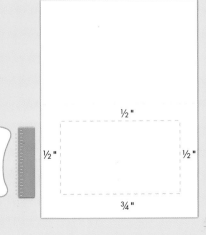

3 The center of the bottom half of the card should now have a rectangle scored into the card that is 5" x 3". Carefully cut this rectangle out, along the score lines, creating a frame on bottom half of the paper.

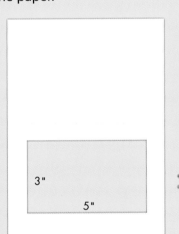

4 Cut out a 2" x 6" piece of matching cardstock, and fold it in half. Unfold it again, and then turn it over and fold in both sides to meet in the middle.

5 Push the folds in to create an accordion shape, like an M, and use the folding tool to crease the folds firmly.

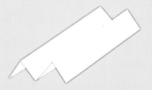

6 Spread glue on both outside edges of the M shape, and attach them to the inside bottom edges of the card.

7 Cut out beach or sports-themed embellishments from the pre-printed patterns, and decorate the outside of your frame. Add glitter glue, gems stickers, or other embellishments if you like.

8 Slide your photo into the frame, resting it in the base of the stand. If you want to change your photo, simply slide out the photo, and slide in a new one!

This absolutely charming set looks challenging to make, but if you follow the steps carefully, it will be a breeze! Once you have it assembled, decorate the set with gems, glitter, ribbons and lace, or anything you can find to enhance this pretty set.

Tea Set

Materials

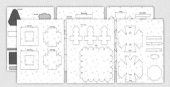
Loose pattern sheets: Tea Set

Ruler

Folding tool

Scissors

Glue

Glitter glue, gems, or other embellishments (optional)

Method

TEAPOT

1 Find the pattern sheets for the tea set. Using a ruler and the folding tool, score lines where the folds will be.

2 Cut out all of the pieces for the teapot and cut the slits in the teapot and lid.

Spout Lid

Handle

Tea Pot

Lid Handle

3 Fold all of the pieces on the score lines you made and crease with the folding tool.

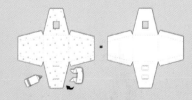

4 Assemble the spout and glue it together.

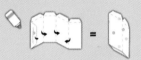

5 Assemble the lid and glue it together. Insert the lid handle into the slit. Flatten the tabs open and glue to them to the underside of the lid to fasten the handle in place.

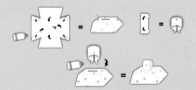

6 Insert the teapot handle tabs into the slits on the side of the teapot, flatten them open and glue them down to the inside of the teapot.

7 Insert the spout in the hole on the front side of the teapot, and flatten the tabs open, gluing them down onto the inside of the teapot to secure the spout in place.

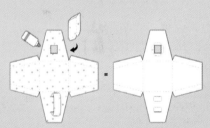

8 Assemble the teapot, gluing the edges down on the tabs to secure them.

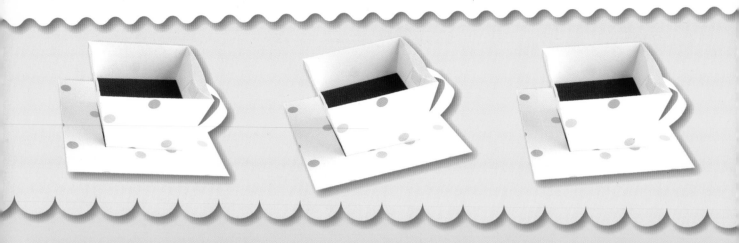

TEACUP

1 On the pattern sheet for the tea cup, score the fold lines with a ruler and folding tool.

2 Cut out the teacup pieces, and cut in the slits in the teacup where the handle is inserted.

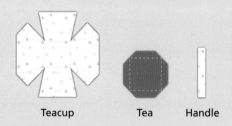

Teacup   Tea   Handle

3 Fold on all of the score lines and crease the folds using the folding tool.

4 Assemble the teacup, gluing the pieces together along the tabs to secure.

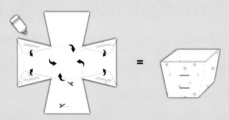

5 Insert the handle tabs into the slits in the teacup and glue the tabs down on the inside of the cup.

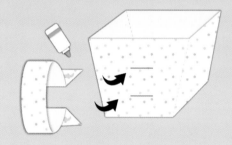

6 Spread glue on the tabs of the tea piece, and insert the tea into the cup, pressing the sides of the cup gently to adhere them to the glued tabs.

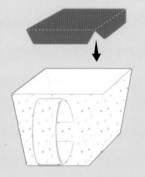

SAUCER

1 On the pattern sheet for the saucer, score the fold lines with a ruler and folding tool.

2 Cut out the pieces and fold on all of the score lines, creasing the folds firmly with the folding tool.

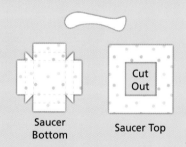

Saucer
Bottom   Saucer Top

3 Assemble the saucer, gluing the tabs to secure the sides.

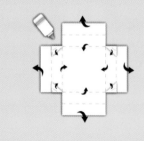

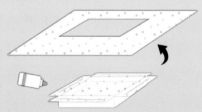

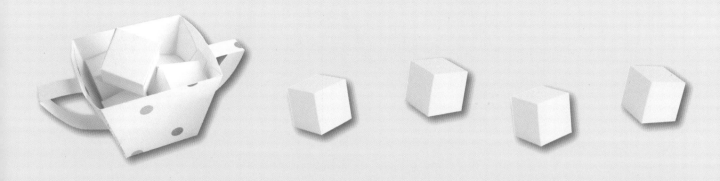

SUGAR DISH

1 Find the pattern sheets for the sugar dish and sugar cubes. Score the fold lines with a ruler and folding tool.

2 Cut out the pieces, including the slits on the side of the dish, and fold on all of the score lines, creasing the folds firmly with the folding tool.

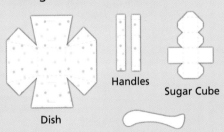

Dish   Handles   Sugar Cube

3 Assemble the sugar dish, spreading glue on the tabs to hold the piece together.

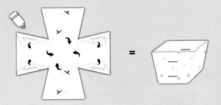

4 Insert the tabs of the handles into the slits on the side of the sugar dish, and flatten them open, gluing them into place.

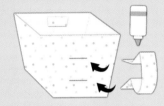

5 Fold the sugar cubes and glue the tabs to keep the pieces together.

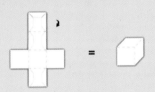

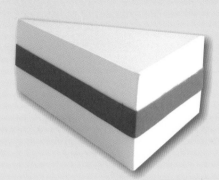

MILK DISH

1 Score the fold lines along the pattern sheet for the milk dish with a ruler and folding tool.

2 Cut out the milk dish pieces and cut in the slits for the handle.

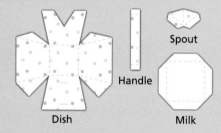

Spout

Handle

Dish

Milk

3 Assemble the milk dish, gluing the tabs to the sides of the piece to secure it.

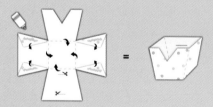

4 Insert the handle tabs into the milk dish and glue them down, securing the handle.

5 Fold the spout piece and attach it to the milk dish, gluing down the tabs.

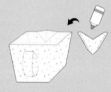

6 Spread glue on the tabs of the milk piece, and insert the milk into the dish, spreading the tabs open and pressing them against the sides of the dish.

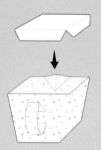

TEA SANDWICH

1 Score the fold lines along the pattern sheet for the tea sandwich with a ruler and folding tool.

2 Cut out the pieces and fold along the score lines, creasing the folds with the folding tool.

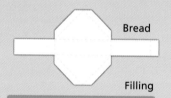

Bread

Filling

3 Assemble the sandwich gluing it together on the tabs.

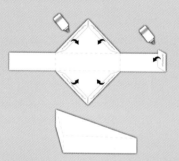

4 Spread glue on the back of the filling strip. Wrap it around the sandwich and hold it carefully for a few seconds to secure it.

CAKE

1 Score the fold lines along the pattern sheet for the cake with a ruler and folding tool.

2 Cut out the cake pieces, and fold along the score lines, creasing the folds with the folding tool.

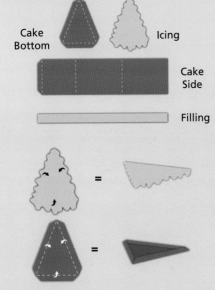

3 Assemble cake sides by gluing the pieces together using the tabs. Glue the cake bottom piece onto the assembled cake sides.

4 Spread glue on back of filling strip and wrap it around the cake slice, pressing it gently until it dries.

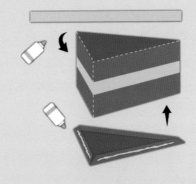

5 Glue the icing piece on top of the cake slice.

PLATE

1 Score the fold lines along the pattern sheet for the plate with a ruler and folding tool.

2 Cut out the plate piece and fold along all of the score lines and crease.

Templates

Cut Lines
Score Lines

Nose
Cut 1

Stripe
Cut 4

Outer Ear
Cut 2

Tooth
Cut 1

Snout
Cut 1

Inner Ear
Cut 2

Bookmark Base
Cut 1

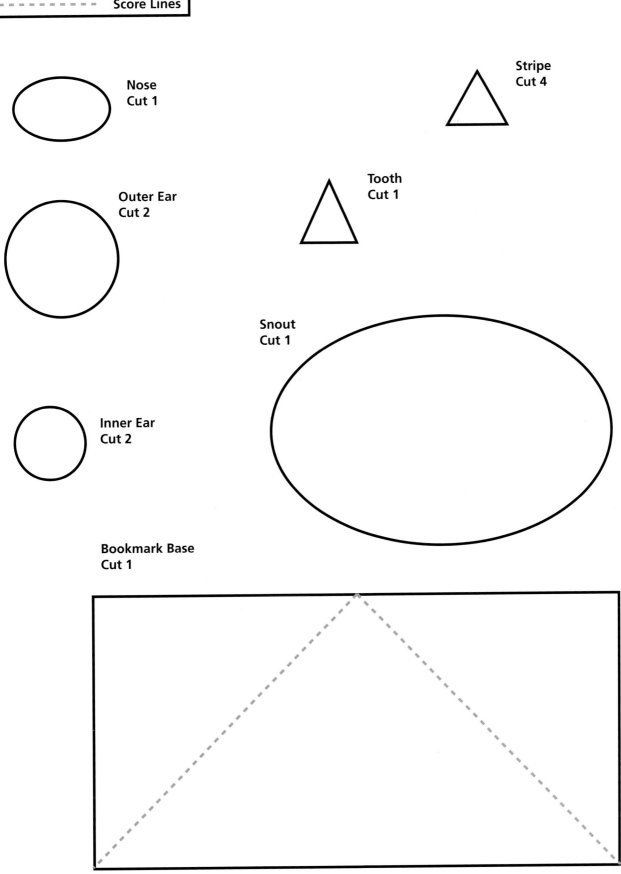

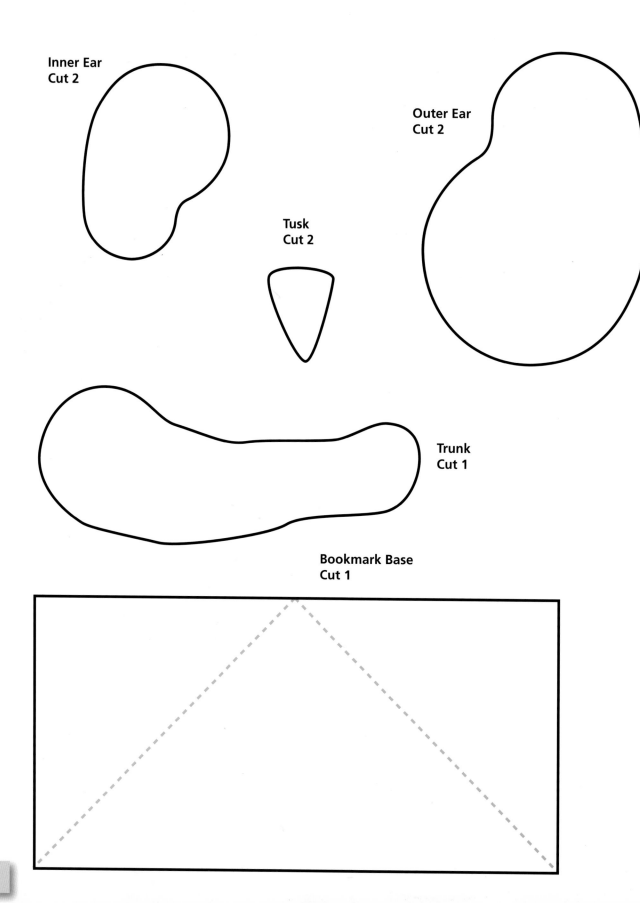

Inner Ear
Cut 2

Outer Ear
Cut 2

Tusk
Cut 2

Trunk
Cut 1

Bookmark Base
Cut 1

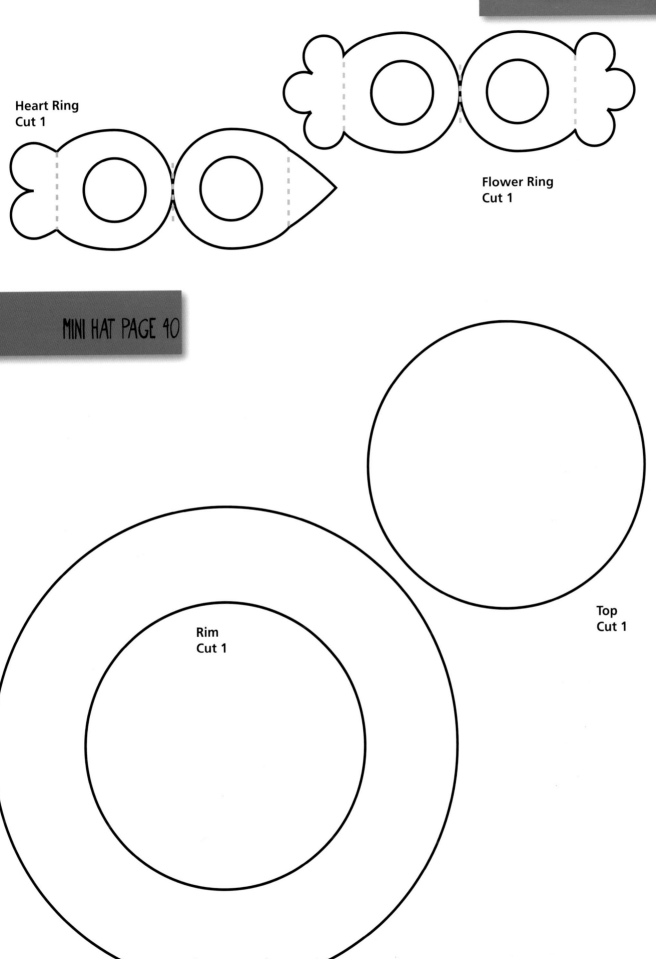

Heart Ring
Cut 1

Flower Ring
Cut 1

MINI HAT PAGE 40

Rim
Cut 1

Top
Cut 1

Face
Cut 1

Hair
Cut 1

Cheek
Cut 2

Smile
Cut 1

Bow
Cut 1

Inner Body
Cut 1

Foot
Cut 2

Bow Tie
Cut 1

Outer Body
Cut 1

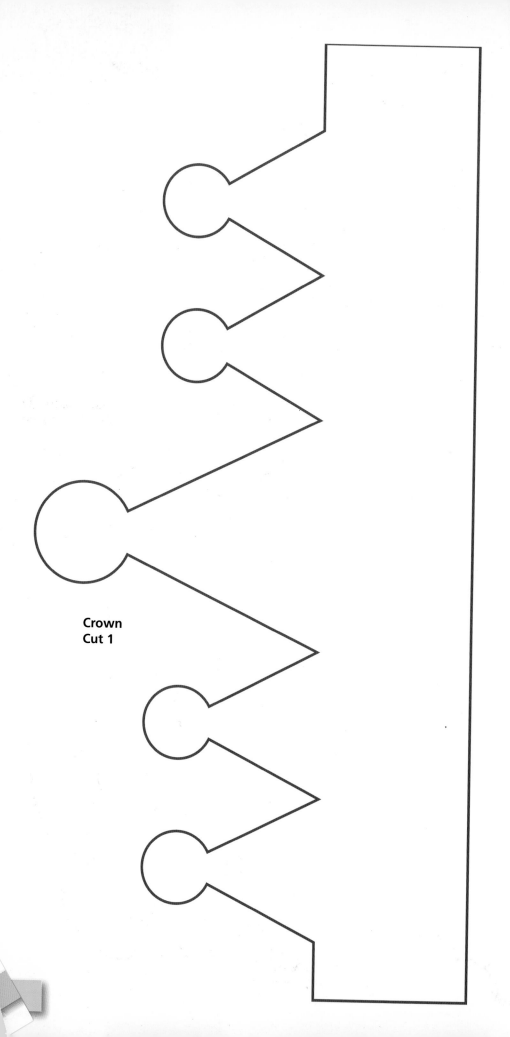

**Crown
Cut 1**